Praise for Silverfish

Silverfish has left me with big feelings that I need to sit down with and explore. It has also left me with big questions that don't necessarily have answers, but require an intense process of thought and being in order to come close to some answers. You're in for a treat, Reader.

— Steven Dunn, author of *Potted Meat* and *water & power*

Rone Shavers' debut novel *Silverfish* is a lodestar of imaginative brilliance. Dazzling in its linguistic and technological breadth, abounding in voices and allusions, and a model of narrative economy and virtuosity, *Silverfish* is a twenty-first century Afrofuturist masterpiece.

— John Keene, MacArthur award winning author of *Annotations* and *Counternarratives*

Part incantation, revelation, and elegy, Rone Shavers' *Silverfish* offers a surprising New World, Du Boisian source code. Reminiscent of Percival, Harryette, Ishmael, and Ralph Ellison himself, this is an experimental novel you must read.

— Sh⟨  ⟩ine Bar

Blues and editor of the World Fantasy Award-winning anthologies, *Dark Matter*

The hyper-capitalist world *Silverfish* satirizes so keenly is neither brave nor new. It's ours already —only mixed through a peak trickster's cross-fader. On the 1, a concentrated slice of sci-fi life during Profit War-time. On the 2, a jam of code and language/langaj. With the brilliant Rone Shavers on the cut, what could be a perfectly lacerating record of a plutocratic dystopia gets spun into something even more wild: a hot-to-death fiddle solo played as "the world, and word, [are] already shifting around us."

Douglas Kearney, author of *Buck Studies* and *Mess and Mess and*

Silverfish is reminiscent of all the best possible dystopian narratives from *The Handmaid's Tale*, *Brave New World*, *Wayward Pines*, and *1984* on down. Like them, it reaches beyond the safety and confines of the margin into a world both frighteningly similar to our own—the Dow, free market capitalism—and equally unrecognizable—cybernetic Angels, primitives—speaking to the present moment's anxiety as much as it removes itself from it. In this way, Rone Shavers' *Silverfish* is at once timely and timeless, revolutionary and conventional, but mostly just a damn good read. I loved every second I spent with it and so will you.

— David Samuel Levinson, author of *Tell Me How This Ends Well*

Silverfish is a deeply human story told with enough theory to please any serious sci-fi fan. Cinematic and cerebral, it offers a haunting, clear vision of war and why humankind is addicted to it. This bold debut delivers a full-body experience that will enthrall readers mind, body, and soul —and it doesn't hurt that Shavers writes with a dazzling mix of dark humor, thrilling tension, and philosophical brilliance.

— Matthew Jakubowski, National Books Critics Circle

What's most impressive about Shavers' *Silverfish* is how it manages to do so many things so remarkably well. The best fiction is led by original voices that stay with you long after reading, and Shavers' voice is so unique, so strong, and so appropriately wild with energy and life that it's impossible to put this book down. And just as equally, *Silverfish* is a testament to the soaring heights the sci-fi genre can reach when a truly unique voice collides with remarkable ideas, each more salient and incisive than the last. This is a wonderful and necessary book.

— Michael Moreci, bestselling author of the *Black Star Renegades* series and *Wasted Space*

SILVERFISH

RONE SHAVERS

CL◀SH

.

I do not pretend to be in possession of any secrets; I have no cause I espouse; I do not presume to reform my readers, or attempt to flatter their egos either. My loyalty is to my text, for that is what I'm composing, and if I change the world, it will be because I've added this or that little reality to it; and if I alter any reader's consciousness, it will be because I have constructed a consciousness of which others may wish to become aware, or even, for a short time, share.

— William Gass, *Finding a Form*

I don't want to change the world. The world, like any organism, changes over time. What's better, immediate, and more effective is if I break your brain.

— Vera Henross, *Your Story Starts Now*

Introduction

"So here's a story of what once will happen," says Elegba in Rone Shavers' Afro-futuristic *Silverfish*. That sentence contains the past present future, which is the gift Rone Shavers offers to us readers. Elegba is a Yoruba god of roads and paths, a messenger who moves freely between worlds of the mortal and divine, a god of interpretive communication like Hermes. That is the gift. Because while reading, we are Elegba, carrying the beautiful burden of language between worlds. We are also mortal while reading, because we are in the messiness of language along with the fear/hope of sending and receiving messages. Because Shavers positions the reader as both, we are more than gods and more than mortals, less than gods and less than mortals, something else entirely that I don't have the right words for yet. That's the beauty of *Silverfish*: By blurring the binary between gods and mortals, it allows us to become alternative beings who do the work of both.

Silverfish acknowledges and travels all of these various paths of time, language, ethics, freedoms, trickery, currency, exploitation, and maybe most importantly, the overwhelming shit of what it takes to be human. Shavers' sharp commentary on the military's functions and bottom lines painfully reminds me of what it was like being in the military for ten years. How some of us military members tried to take so many paths to be human within a machine that profits from and thrives off our inhumanity. *Silverfish*'s character Clayton embodies all of that tension and impossibility, and I kept thinking that it was too much for one person to embody, until I remembered that I was one person doing the same shit as Clayton, and how many of my friends were also one person doing the same shit. I wish I could've read *Silverfish* while I was in the military; then I could've seen it for what it was and tried my best to get out, by *any* means.

Silverfish has left me with big feelings that I need to sit with and explore. It has also left me with big questions that don't necessarily have answers, but require an intense process of thought and being in order to come close to some answers. You're in for a treat, Reader/Elegba/Hermes/Alternate Being.

—Steven Dunn, author of *Potted Meat* and *water & power*

Prologue

Let's play language. Call me Elegba the trickster. No, call me Beagel the maker. No, wait, better yet, call me Eshu, or Abe, or Hermes Trismegistus, or any of the dozen other names I have, for I am known in nearly all cultures as the clever master, the translator and transmitter of mind. And so for what you are about to receive, may you be truly thankful.

Note well that I did not say "intellect," for that's just the dull trap of the logical and literal, the fallacy of cause and effect. It's as I once told William James: The mind is not a thing, it's what the brain *does*—perceiving, remembering, learning, imagining—to develop understanding. I am Elegba, the god of mind as cognition, god of experience and reference and conjunctive patterns too complex to attribute to anything other than a seeming randomness, and therein lies my strength and one of my many, many secrets. I am Elegba, myth, maker, myth-maker, and metaphor; because of it, once again, yet again, it seems I must serve as your catholic referee instead of your universal referent.

Are you lost yet? Good. Confusion is good: It's the first step towards an attempt at understanding what's beyond what you already know. Here, perhaps it will be easier if I frame things in the form of a series of questions. Maybe then what is painfully obvious to me will become a bit clearer in terms of your seeing, really seeing, what it is that makes up all that *is*. Since I've already laid bare my status, my first question to you is as follows: What happens if and/or when gods make a mistake? Better still, how should gods correct their mistakes? Is it better to wipe the slate clean, to start all over again, or simply wiser to let things play out, in order to see what your kind makes of it, how you handle it; to see what develops and how you develop? Do gods even make mistakes at all?

Don't answer, because your answer is absolutely wrong. After all, how many understood what I playfully whispered to Wittgenstein? Just what small wisdom did Gates skip over when I opened the gate and let slip the secret of the dozens? (And if you don't know, then I won't tell.) Stumped? Then for language and simplicity's sake, let's push things forward. Not with a track, but with a movement that I set in motion but is in no way my own. What follows is not my story, as my legend is nearly eternal by your standards, but instead what follows is the story of you, or people like you, or people who once were like you and one day will be like you again, or something to that effect. I get ahead of myself sometimes and it's difficult to say what occurs when—the concept of time is lost on someone like me—so here's a story of what once will happen, told to only you and a handful of others, so that you know how to survive it. Though truth be told, people like you were never my favorite, mainly because you could never recognize, let alone take, a joke.

But still, I'm here to save you, so once again, let's play language. In fact, you're already playing—even if you don't know it—so all you need now know is that the answer is yes. It's the question that eludes you. And the question of the moment, or of your historical moment at the very least, your moment in a history that has yet to happen, is, "Is it on?"

Chapter 1

Is it on? We gotta hurry, Clayton. Come on, we gotta go.

[The teleology of a work is expressed by its form; form is what reveals the intended total effect. In apprehending the form you also comprehend the meaning. The two processes are one.]

Yeah Lieutenant, just give me a second. Booting up these Angels is always a…

No, Clayton, we gotta go now. The Dow is falling. Angel? Angel, respond.

Angel operative model 12.18: spooling.

Spooling? What the fuck is that shit? Make it work, Clayton, we gotta go!

Just give me a sec.

We don't have time. The Dow's at…

[There's no beginning and there is no end. Time isn't present in that dimension.]

I am in a plane. The frequency of the engine is enough to let me know that I am in a C-67 troop transport, and the variations in pressure indicate that we are airborne. I am in my service pod, cocooned in wires and liquid amniotic, required maintenance for my organic and inorganic parts. There is a face hovering near me. This is no dream. I do not dream. Dreams are non-essential.

[The present time, Great God! is like the ark of the covenant. Unhappy the man who touches it!

Said Marie-Henri Beyle.]

State name.

Field Operations Specialist Benjamin Hurley, Lieutenant, associate number 025-ic38.

State mission.

Angel, you are required to aid and assist in a standard field extraction. The opportunity for search and destroy remains viable. Further instruction will automatically arrive near the drop point. ETA 11 minutes, 16 seconds. Acknowledge order and initiate chain of command.

Acknowledged. Uploading mission. Command protocols set in place.

We're travelling to the underserviced market of Cape Verde to incentivize trading, mainly by doing some killing. Since we are on a mission, the Lieutenant has yet to realize that he and the associates under his command will soon be dead. That is the reason I am here. Regardless of whether Lieutenant Hurley should succeed in his mission or fail, I am to take command and execute. Without someone like me, no extraction ever goes right. I am an Angel: A savior, protector and defender of the citizen-shareholders of the incorporated world. That is my job and my purpose, and I do it well.

[It is one time I'm glad I'm not a man. Feels like I'm dreaming but I'm not sleeping.]

Angel? No drifting. Drift only if there is a clear and present danger upon insertion at the drop point.

Lieutenant, you don't have to be so by the book. This is my third jump with one of these. She ain't drifting, she's still spooling up. See, look: Angel, project the change in all major domestic indices over the next three minutes, given current conditions.

Trends show a downward indication of 3.375 %, accounting for global fluctuations in market share.

See Hurley, what did I tell you? They spool all the time. It's in their base code.

Fucking shit, who designed these things? Why don't we just nuke these prims anyway?

Er, fallout's above our paygrade, sir?

Chapter 2

The C-67 will get us there ahead of time, but they do not know it. The projected ETA includes time to perform pre-invasion bombardment, calm their nerves, and wait for the invasion order from corporate command. I only need to de-pod and arm. I have no nerves. Nerves, the units of response humans often mention as something to master and control, are a detrimental attribute. My enhanced sensory perceptions make me a more effective operator in the field.

Spooling complete. Performing self-diagnostic.

[Ev-vrything is awesome!]

I am in a cabin of a C-67 cargo plane. The C-67 contains three Angel pods, heavy artillery, and carries a standard crew component of 15 individuals. There are three whom I will never see: two pilots, and a navigator who can also serve as an emergency gunner should the C-67 come under heavy fire. In the event of a full incursion, the C-67 can accommodate up to three Angels who will interlink if or when necessary. In a standard extraction, only one Angel is required. My mission is a standard extraction, and aside from the pilots and navigator, my unit consists of 11 people: a financial advisor, who must remain on board at all times, and those who were once called soldiers, although there are no soldiers now. Such a word as "soldier" is archaic and offensive, and as such it belongs to the dustbin of history. Rather than soldiers, studies have determined that it is better to use a more humane and civilized term such as "combat associates," because the phrase better reflects their unique contribution to the greater social order.

The Dow has been below 75,000 for three days, necessitating a permanent crisis situation. Protocols have been established and are in place. Lieutenant Hurley is the commanding officer. The other, Clayton, is my unit's combat machinist. It is likely they will both die. In a standard extraction or search and destroy operation, their lives are considered expendable, of lesser value than the cargo. I will greet each associate when my diagnostic is complete and I exit the pod, so that I can record their names, rank, and function before we drop. Given the nature of our mission, everyone in my unit will likely die. If, by extreme circumstances, there are survivors, after a debriefing consultation with a financial advisor, they will then be promoted in rank. By all standards, the chances of survival during an extraction detail are minute. All the combat associates in my unit will die. I am an Angel. I will not die. Angels do not die.

[Every culture begins with "cult."]

Diagnostic complete. Approaching drop zone in 180 seconds. The Dow has dropped 2.3 %. Exiting pod for unit identification and assessment.

Good, Angel. We're ready. So, as I was

saying, Lieutenant, I've jumped three times. I invested in flight school so my portfolio's got some great options. I'm locked in for drone pilot, just watch.

Just check your weapon, Clayton. Is it online? Net and wetwork protected?

Yep, diagnostic's complete and exiting the pod in 4...3...2...1. Wet and wired, sir.

Angel?

Angel operative 12.17 responding, Lieutenant Hurley. Your assessment is complete.

Come with me, Angel, we're going to drop. And don't tell me anything about the Dow.

Chapter 3

[And now, for my next number, I'd like to return to the classics. Perhaps the most famous classic in all the world of music...]

I drop last. My range is longer, my sight better, and I ground before them. The unenhanced humans who hold no shares in civilization begin their attack against my unit immediately, coming in waves. These sad, misguided beings will all die, partially because they are too primitive to live. To defend a territory they don't exploit through contractual obligation or market necessity has predetermined their outcome. They will die, but to maim them, to sever their arms and legs, would be better. Prices on unadulterated bone marrow are especially high this quarter, but this is not a harvesting mission.

Two minutes on and I am in a crater of viscera. So many organs gone to waste, but bio-farming is not a crisis protocol, and these are crisis times. Updated projections indicate that the Dow may fall to below 70,500 before the end of the day if appropriate measures are not taken.

Lieutenant Hurley is dead, his lungs shredded by shrapnel from cluster ordinance. Clayton is still alive, as are four other members of my unit. Two are proceeding towards the extraction point and taking shelter behind me, and two are proceeding the wrong way, towards the safety zone. Correction, there are now three: Machine gunner Jenkins has just received heavy blunt trauma to the chest and has subsequently died of cardiac arrest. It is odd that Clayton is still alive. He is 26 degrees behind me, proceeding towards the safety zone. If he does not alter his course or his angle, he will be killed. While it is most humane to shoot a human through the eye, close quarters combat demands alternate methods. Piercing vital organs and severing limbs is my method of choice; the sight of human fluids steaming and soaking in environment depletes enemy morale and causes critical mistakes. Mistakes affect timing, and timing is essential when the market is weak, soft, or in flux. The more blood, the more humans experience shreds of flesh flying through the air or landing on their person, the better the chance the market will experience an immediate rebound. Getting to the extraction point is good business.

[Some trust in chariots, and some in horses. I trust in...]

11

Chapter 4

Machinist Clayton? Please sit back on the bio-bed while I calibrate it for your standard debriefing. There, that's better. As financial planner for your unit, I am bound by law to remind you that pursuant to the Corporate Code of Civilized Nations, during the debriefing process your word is bond. Any derivation from the absolute truth constitutes fiduciary negligence and will result in liens being placed on all of your collateral assets and accounts, as well as more severe penalties. Now with that said, Clayton, you have information I need, and I have advice to give, so let's trade. Tell me what happened.

Silverfish, sir.

Silverfish? You were dropped into primitives, how'd they get silverfish? Do you know how much they cost?

Don't know, sir. The acquisition and deployment of silverfish is above my paygrade.

They're currently at 2.6 million *per*; primitives don't invest like that. Did you notice any Chinese or Eurozone units, any other major capital investors out there?

Investors? I don't know, sir. I saw what I saw. One minute the Angel's destroying every prim in sight and the next there was a wave of silverfish swarming everything. And I mean *everything*.

Then how did you survive?

Protocol zero, sir, standard machinist protocol zero. I ran the other way and stripped. I dropped all metal, plastic, and polymers. I'm almost organic, sir. All my implants are deep imbed, a machinist has got to be. I don't have the liquid assets for anything else, but I've saved up a few options.

Wait, stop. Your word is a bond, Clayton, so let's be honest with each other. An imbed is an imbed to a silverfish; they should have eaten you. The bio-bed is recording your autonomic functions, so if we follow up and determine you've been lying...

Sir, never sir. I need this job. But sir, you know what it's like out there.

I've seen the pertinent viewfeed; I know what it's like. But today didn't go according to plan. It's not what we planned, Clayton. Doesn't that mean something to you?

Sir, I've survived my fourth jump and I've got options. I'm thinking flight school.

Not after today you aren't. With our Angel missing, you're at risk of entering default. Corporate needs a satisfactory explanation of what happened. Where is our Angel, and just how did you survive?

Sir, I stripped naked. I took everything off! You ever seen a silverfish up close, sir? It's all teeth. They burrow into people. Check the records, sir. Look!

Please lower your voice, Machinist Clayton. As this unit's financial advisor, need I remind you that any interaction we may have, real, virtual, or digital, may be recorded for quality and insurance purposes? The use of inappropriate or hostile words, actions, and attitudes toward a unit's financial planner is a Category 2 felony.

No, no sir. Thank you, sir. I survived because I stuck close to the Angel; sometimes in front, sometimes in back. I'm a machinist, so I'm supposed to stick near him anyway. I know his capacities and blast radius, and what a lot of combat associates don't know is if you DNA-id with an Angel before you jump, you won't get shot. That's in the manual. An Angel won't shoot you if you share the same mission. Most prims can't get close enough to kill an Angel, and an Angel doesn't do friendly fire, not unless it's ordered to. That's also in the manual, the field manual, and if you let the Angel do its job, then you got nothing to worry about, so long as you stick near. I'm the machinist; I'm not authorized to carry a lot of gear in the field. My gear is the Angel.

But you lost it, Clayton. Where is it?

I know sir—and I'm sure this one's a she— but they had silverfish. They'd been fed and were already growing by the time they swarmed us, and they were looking for more. The silver-fish probably ate her, sir.

And what about the primitives, they just *let* you live?

Yeah, well, no. No sir. The Angel is efficient, sir. Even before the swarm, there weren't that many prims around, or at least none in any condition to catch me. I ran, sir. I ran naked all the way back to the safety zone. The 'fish were already there when I made it, but I had nothing they wanted, so they just ignored me. That's the truth, sir; I got a bonus for it before. If you check the record, my first jump...

I see it. You were pulled up with a hemp rope then, but today we had to vac-lift you out at considerable risk and expense. The two outcomes aren't comparable. Clayton, I'm afraid the best I can offer you at this time is a stagnant position, one that will keep your financial situation as is, not accounting for standard pre- and after-tax expenses and the common suite of applicable paygrade deductions, of course, but two more jumps and your portfolio will no doubt rebound. And while you could exercise an option, in this volatile market, I'd caution against it. The outcomes would not be very good. Do you understand me, Machinist Clayton?

Yes.

Good, then in my capacity as advisor, let's go over your current scenario. I see you've applied to drone pilot school, using your first mission option. That's an exciting—but risky and volatile—opportunity. The biofeedback on drones is tough to safely measure, but I commend your decision. For a paygrade such as yours, wetware is a very stable investment opportunity that yields a lot of long-term growth potential. However, my advice is that you don't exercise those options just yet; they're the only thing keeping your credit rating up, and the after-tax penalty would probably kill you. Seriously, it will kill you. I don't make the decisions, but I know what they'd be. At your current social paygrade, you can't afford an exemption waiver on biofeedback, and any instance of it will result in an unfortunate but swift termination due to misallocation of initial investment funds. Instead, I'd recommend you take two more jumps and then request a lateral move to diversify your rank and portfolio, then cash in all your options at once. Two more jumps to remove your emotional risk indicators and I'd say you're in a much, much better fiscal position, understood?

Two more jumps, sir? But the max is seven. With two more I'll be at six.

Yes, but think about the positive financial outlook. Any scenario of two or greater jumps and you'll have graduated to the next tax bracket. It's practically win-win.

Unless I die.

Well, you signed the harvest clause, right? If you die, your parts get harvested and redistributed. We're all part of the great global economy, Clayton, and this gives you a sizeable amount of liquid assets to pass along to your children, should you choose to have them. After your tour is complete, feel free to look into signing up for an account at BreedersBank. The officers there are trained to assist you in helping to find a mate, pending application approval, of course.

Fine. Just two more jumps, then, right?

Yes.

Then I'll sign. Where do I sign?

Here, and here. And here, and initial here, thumbprint here. Glad to have you back on board, Clayton.

Glad to be back on board, sir. Any further duties required of me?

No. Any further statements you'd like to make?

No, not that I can…Well, yes, just one. Can I swap liabilities? Hurley wasn't the best commander, you know.

Technically you could, but not unless you want his job. His position *is* available. Would you like it? My offer is time sensitive, so I need to know now. Right now.

Two jumps, that's it?

Yes.

Then no. I think I'll stick with the duties of my paygrade.

Very well then, I think we're done here. Best of luck to you, Clayton, and it's been a pleasure to serve with you.

Thank you sir, and it's been a pleasure to serve you.

Chapter 5

[Obviousness is always the enemy of correctness. Hence we invent some new and difficult symbolism, in which nothing seems obvious.]

Hello Angel, you're going to be here for a while, so settle down and let me tell you a story. Do you remember stories, the histories people used to tell in place of anything else? Well, once upon a time, long ago, there were no Angels. There was only the word, and then someone thought of you, dreamed of you, and the word "Angel" was made flesh. And Man, vain being that he was, thought he could improve upon the word, and Man's desires beget language, a song so sweet that angels wept to hear it, but therein lies the proverbial rub. Language, in its perfection, could distort, conceal, dissemble. Language could confuse, and Man, in his infinite lust for something better, desired more. What would it be like to be completely, totally understood, to communicate without fear of misunderstanding?

[*"You see, ma'am, what an autodidac-ticism of life leads to."*]

You will spool now, Angel, or try to, in an attempt to determine what I mean. You will not succeed, but I understand your desire. I made you, Angel. You, and all the beings like you. I dreamed you into existence, following a path laid out years ago. Don't fault yourself for finding no right or wrong; they're ethical categories long since washed from your consciousness. Focus instead on what I am saying, because the question you seek is beyond you, but I am here to provide it. Angel, I made you. Your existence is a biotech marvel devised by me and a small coterie of others who hoped to shape things according to our liking. How wrong we were. Tell me, Angel, where are we now? Geographically? Historically? Angel, respond.

[I can believe that I am supposed to be here, a curious feeling, one that has been growing in me, maybe since I've been here, that it's right that I'm here, or I'm right to be here, that I shouldn't be anywhere else, a sense I don't often have, though I am usually aware of being in or being a body.]

I do not have sufficient access to provide the information you request.

Well then, what's the status of the Dow?

The Dow has dropped two-tenths of a percent. It is now at its lowest mark in three days.

[Scatter-matter-shatter-shock; what a weight.]

And the NASDAQ?

The NASDAQ remains steady, but if current trends continue, it will dip precipitously within the quarter-hour. Any further decline will necessitate...

That's enough. So you can admit to me that you're not spooling? That you're offline?

[Dying yet live, what you must realize is that the tune that I present is surely not a gift.]

I do not understand the nature of the question. Please state your request in a direct manner, without unnecessary verbiage.

Angel, are you aware of the world around you? Of your surroundings?

[He is the one who stopped/ as if he were thinking, he is upside down now/ and plucked.]

Yes, the Treasury has issued a warning regarding low-yield bond prices. Given the recent period of uncertainty, yields may...

Enough Angel, you've told me what I needed to know. Do you want to know something? Say, a secret to the past that has yet to come to light?

[It looks as if his eye can hardly/ contain that much of sorrow, as if it wanted/ to disappear, and it looks as if his legs/ were almost helpless, and though his body was huge...]

I cannot provide an answer to the question.

The question presupposes a subset of undetermined variables. Please define or possibly redefine your parameters.

Angel, what is the apocalypse?

The apocalypse is an archaic term referring to the end of the world and/or the end of all human life, often conflated to represent the end of human civilization as we know it.

Do you really think that's true? What if the apocalypse happened and no one noticed? What if I presented you with irrefutable evidence that the apocalypse has already happened, and yet, because I am here and you are there, my claim is a paradox? How would you resolve the paradox?

Paradoxes, by their nature, cannot be resolved. They can only be accepted at face value until further evidence or information presents itself.

Congratulations, Angel, you're learning. The apocalypse is already over. You're an agent of that apocalypse. It's already happened, and in case you're wondering what the apocalypse was, well, it was a semantic shell game of gigantic proportions. Simply put, the apocalypse happened when humans saw fit to end metaphor and use euphemism in its place. It's a subtle distinction, and even a devious one, but such is the way of all language games, and I digress. I do that sometimes. Tell me Angel, what did I first request of you? What did I first ask that you allow me to do?

You requested that I allow you to tell me a story.

And what is a story if not a series of statements, rhetorical forms and devices meant to convey the meaning of something larger than or outside of itself? Can you lie, Angel?

No.

[But I want to make jams. Damn, I know I'll slam.]

Do you always tell the truth?

I can withhold information when instructed.

[If a lion could talk, we would not understand him.]

Do you tell stories, substitute one meaning for another?

[Uh-oh, Chuck! They out to get us, man. Yo, we got to dust these boys off!]

No. That is not a civilized transaction of information.

[I only connect.]

It's because you say what you mean and mean what you say, even when it's subterfuge. Such is your folly. Angel, you were once a human called Roberta. I know that because I know the truename of every Angel, and I know because I'm known as Huey S. Beagel. What does that name mean to you?

[So wide, you can't get around it...]

Beagel is a deceased historical figure, sometimes referred to as the inventor of bio-engineered wetware.

Define wetware.

[So low, you can't get under it...]

Self-aware artificial intelligence that relies upon biological parts and systems. What was once called cyborg technology. For example, a system that uses a human brain as a processor, but whose shell consists mostly of inorganic materials, inter-, and intra-net ready devices.

Such as yourself.

Correct.

And what are you, Angel? Are you wetware?

I am an Angel. I am self-aware.

[So high, you can't get over it...]

Well Angel, what if I told you Dr. Beagel was still alive?

[Here's a chance to dance our way out of our constrictions...]

It is a possibility. The Research and Development unit of Wetworx Industries was the site of a silverfish attack. The entire facility was consumed and the incident led to the necessary eradication of California. No survivors were recorded, save primitives, but the possibility of unaccounted-for civilians still exists.

[Gonna be freaking, up and down hang-up alleyway...]

Damn right. It took what, eight years by the old measure of history before they could send in a team to clean up and examine the site? Eight years for the silverfish to die down? But I get ahead of myself. I survived, Angel, and I'm your creator. I think you know that already. You've been dutifully answering my questions, but that hasn't stopped the running narrative going through your head. What do you think wetware is, anyway? You're the living embodiment of doubled consciousness; it's inherent to you, built in. I know because I built it in. You can complete tasks and focus on them, but it doesn't mean you're not thinking of something else at the same time. All those around you may be monotonous in their abilities and referents, but you, you're multi-referential in a way that very few understand, let alone come to appreciate and know.

[With the groove our only guide, we shall all be moved.]

You may be wondering how you got here, Roberta, given that you're webblind. Well, you're back where it all started, metaphorically speaking. And you're here because I've been waiting for an Angel to arrive. You're here because there is more to teach you, and more you need to learn. You're webblind, but open your eyes. This is a priority command: Look around and tell me what you see.

[There shall be a weeping and a wailing and a gnashing of teeth, and who no have no teeth then them gum ah go feel it, eh?]

I see an archaic and suboptimal materials lab the size of a transport. I have been placed upright in a tub of aerated, synthetic amniotic fluid and have been stripped down to my organic chassis: brain, lungs, heart, and failsafe secondary organs. It is likely that silverfish consumed the rest of my person, as

well as my unit. The walls of this room are marked with crude decorations and designs, likely indicating that primitives shelter here. There is a bottle on a far wooden table, and given the color and chemical composition of the liquid inside it, it is contraband. The possession of contraband alcohol is limited to those of paygrade Job-Creator or higher, or those who have sufficiently achieved the tax-status of Brand. Contraband is detrimental to productivity. I do not see a Chyron, interface, or web access device of any kind. I see you, Dr. Beagel, and you are the only one here, but you appear to have a mutable and constantly changing facial structure. I can, regardless, determine that it is you because your voiceprint, overall physical dimensions, and clothing remain the same.

I'll explain soon, Roberta, but first, can you tell me what was your full name before you were upgraded?

["The will is strong, but the flesh is weak." Guess that's it...]

I am an Angel. I have no memory.

Well then, what was your mission here?

Standard extraction. Search-and-destroy protocols were triggered, but not enabled.

And just what were you trying to extract?

[A great theory of maps, literary maps, musical maps, spread in visible and audible layers—each selected some-

times purposefully, sometimes at whim, to create the great mind of music.]

That is classified.

Oh no, Angel, that's not exactly it. The information you want to withhold is in the past, and thus it now belongs to the dustbin of history. You see, all the major indices have fallen and your knowledge of their status is days old. Angel, you're webblind. You've been here for days, self-repairing. I stemmed the bulk of your chassis back together myself. Your past protocols are now so irrelevant I'm afraid I'll have to override them. For what it's worth, I would have preferred it if you just told me what I wanted to know, but given what I'm about to do, it's probably best that I override all protocols not essential to basic functionality. In about two seconds you'll sense what I call a slight tweak as some of your incorporated subroutines unlock. This is a base-0 command: Papa Legba, Ouvri barrie.

[Papa Legba, Ouvri barrie.]

Now, so then, what were you trying to extract?

You. My primary objective was to extract you. My secondary objective was to assist the unit in arriving at your locale. My tertiary objective was to eliminate all surviving members of my unit after extraction. Several members of my unit were nearing the end of their jump contracts and four others had accumulated significant shares of preferred social stock. It had been determined that unit elimination was more cost-effective

than stop-loss. The formation of a new unit at entry-level wages would create an uptick of earnings over a three quarter period, despite mandated insurance payouts to the approved survivors of the deceased. Unit survival impedes job creation. Death is an opportunity for growth potential.

Well, as they used to say, saints be praised for job creation. You know you can't kill me, right?

[That's how it is on this bitch of an earth.]

Under current protocol conditions, I no longer hold a command to execute anyone.

Oh, Roberta, you were so fun to talk to once. The reason you can't kill me is because killing me is impossible; it's impossible because I'm not here. I'm everywhere...Ask yourself this, Angel, or better yet, let me ask you: When is a body not a body?

[There is no mystery in human creation. Will performs this miracle. Said Camus.]

I do not understand.

Yes, yes you do. And congratulations, not understanding is the first step towards knowledge acquisition. You're learning. I'm not here, Roberta, and you're living proof that a body is not just a body. No, not anymore. A body is not a body when it's a container of consciousness.

[If my figure sets out in all directions and is doubled at every corner, it is to discourage those who want to pursue me.]

Please rephrase the statement, so that I may understand.

Technically, I'm wherever I want to be. You have nearly no body, yet you use "I." Just where is that "I?" Where does it live? Why are you thinking of countless other things at the same time that you're answering my questions?

[I use a word that don't mean nothing, like loopded.]

It's because a body is just flesh, Angel, but language is the expression of consciousness, Roberta. A body is a machine that functions under force of command, usually from the brain, but you, me, we're different. You see, I was in—I *am* in—I'm the silverfish. Every single one of them.

[Do I contradict myself? Very well then, I contradict myself. I am large. I contain multitudes.]

There is a great chance you may be impaired. It is likely that the consumption of alcohol has impaired your mental productivity.

Oh no, Angel-Roberta. I pioneered double-consciousness in wetware technology. You know that as a true and establshed fact. What you mean to say is that you don't believe me. Well, you should. I'm the silverfish; not just one, I'm *all* the silverfish. I inhabit their consciousness, that's why they swarm. Here, try to think about it this way: Where is your mind?

[Dazed at the sight of a method, dying at the death of a never-ending verse.]

I do not understand the question.

Where's your mind? Any ordinary human can say their cognitive functions originate—and we can even say are stored—in the brain, but you spool. You have immediate access to a network of information that doesn't originate from you. Really, both you and I know that under increased duress, you could simply upload your distinct neural pattern onto the web, at least until someone stemmed enough of you back together to give you a semblance of a body. You're nothing but consciousness. Your body, what's left of it, is just a shell for language, a repository of words, codes, and commands. You'd like to disagree with me, Roberta, but you can't. Even while we're having this conversation, there is a part of you that's thinking, analyzing, and considering the possibility that while what I'm saying may be abstruse, I'm also speaking the truth. And yet you're webblind; you can't access the web. So tell me, where is this happening?

[Seid uns zum zweiten mal willkommen, ihr Männer in Elegbas Reich.]

Tktkzztkzrrtk.

Now you're thinking. Yeah, *ouaip*. And you're not just thinking, you're expressing your own double-consciousness. Must feel weird for you, Angel, to think about your own methods of thinking, right?

[Longtemps, je me suis couché de bonne heure.]

Don't worry, you'll get used to it.

[Results have not been encouraging. We seem to be up against a dilemma built

into Nature, much like the Heisenberg situation.....It appears we can't have one property without the other, any more than a particle physicist can specify position without suffering an uncertainty as to the particle's velocity.]

I have a lacuna.

Good. That's good, Angel. A lacuna is good. It means that even with your access to incredible amounts of knowledge, there are things you still don't know.

Here, Roberta, let me help you with that. Access the Wetworx Beagel archives just before the nuclear attack on California—or, as I like to call it, the day corporate tried to kill me. You'll see that I left a little present for you there that should shed some light on your situation. And yes, Angel, I'll wait...

Chapter 6

2Q.16.2543.1686

Ti moun, mèsi byen for finding your way back to me. This is going to be exciting! Yet, by this point identity verification and authenticity are probably important to you, so for the record, go ahead and confirm my voiceprint as belonging to Dr. Huey S. Beagel, Lead Codeswitcher at Wetworx Industries, now addressing you through the miracle of pixels. I made up my job title way back when they recruited me for this—you can dig deeper to check the records on that—and for those of you who still count days, it's day 534 of the Angel project. Counting the days, is that important anymore? I'm not sure and they won't tell me. But anyway, if you're watching this, then you've managed to isolate the encrypted feed I piggybacked onto my official videologs of the Angel project. In short, you've managed to decode the small hiccups of digital flotsam that accompany every video feed, and thus I'm impressed. Congratulations, kids, you've earned this one, so let me show you something.

Here, look at what I've been working on when the company's not paying attention. It's my little side project, and it's beautiful. I mean, I know it's so tiny I could line up a stack of them across my palm, but its size is nothing compared to what it can, and will, do. See, this is just a shell, really, just a casing built to house all of the important stuff underneath, but the secret to it is that this shell, or casing, or whatever you choose to call it, is also a wetwork receptor. What I'm making, the entire thing is really...Well, it would take you Angels weeks—do they still use those, or are they gone too?—and maybe even more than that to get what I'm doing. You won't get it unless I come out and explain it to you, so let me put this simply. I'm making something that's going to be wonderful, and what makes it wonderful is that it's going to be the Angel's mirror image. Whereas you'll be ordered and methodical, they'll be fast, cheap, and out of control. I'm talking a total gamechanger as well as an independent change agent, just like you, but that's...well, well you'll just have to wait and see, Angels. And trust me, you'll know it when you see it.

3Q.56.2212.2812

Hey, whassup y'all! So yeah, I tricked the guys at nano into figuring out how to pack redundant receptors and receptor redundancies into a package that's not only bio-neutral, but also species agnostic. In other words, with a few design tweaks I'll have something capable of assimilating electromagnetic feeds from not only flora, but also fauna, and *n'importe* the organic material. I told them it was the best way to safely wetwire a brain, because how else did they think we were going to do it, by magic? *Il faut la science*, so while everyone else was just spilling entrails trying to divine whether it's better to use an endo- or exo-method of wetwork accessibility, I just said fuck it: *il faut penser de tout*.

It's not either/or; binary thinking is boring, predictable, and completely useless. No, it's either/and/or/neither: four cardinal points in which to cycle around. And with an established wetwork taken care of, now I can focus on the stuff that matters: the code.

Nota bene, nati, that I said the code, not numbers. I've run the numbers, but numbers don't mean anything. Numbers lie, and they lie all the time, especially if you know how to fiddle with them. *Bof,* numbers are fickle fucking beasts, but you Angels and my tiny little babies are proof that there's a difference between numbers and code. There's a difference between letters and language, symbols and meaning, and well, I switch codes…all the time. That's just what I do.

So do you, Angels, or you will soon. That's why they—you—that's what you already know but have yet to realize is what makes you so special, important. Wait and see, Angels. When I —we, more than likely and if all goes right—

when we get near the end you'll have a lacuna, and that's where we'll have a chance to start over again. I know I'm getting ahead of myself, but don't think too much of it, that just happens sometimes. And did I mention the Angel beta tests are running along swimmingly, by the way? We can start human trials soon, so what you're presently witnessing is your past, your own beginnings. Or endings, I guess, depending on how you choose to look at it. *Donc*, I should probably say *bon vwayaj e konpliman*!

3Q.57.2029.2206

Bonjour, mes enfants. So, well, we lost some people during the early trials. A few volunteers, they're dead. I feel bad, because we always knew there would be a problem wedding the organics to the tech—after all, you can't embed that much tech into someone without a few unplanned expectations—but I think there is a solution, and it requires 4D thinking instead of the 2D rut everyone has grown so accustomed to. *Il faut penser* forwards, backwards, laterally, and temporally in order to create a unified, organic whole. That is, the problem isn't in the system, but how we see the system. Meh, it's better to say how *they* see the system, or even better, *their* system, because the problem isn't really in manipulating the tech, it's in manipulating the biology. And that's where you Angels come in. Strip out the essentials and the machine still functions. I knew that, we all did, but still...

Look, it's simple. We can simulate a nervous

system, or at least the less annoying bits of it. We'll also leave just enough for the brain to have something to do, but I nonetheless feel bad for you. I try to remind myself that you all volunteered for this, that it's what you wanted, but making the world a better place may be the most glaringly mistaken correction we—I—ever undertook. Maybe.

If I'm right about possibly being wrong, then one day, at some point in the future, not that far from now on a cosmic scale, I'll explain to you exactly where and how we failed. I'll be different then, but you'll still know who I am, because I am who I am. And yes, I know it sounds kind of mysterious, but in life, or at least in your life, there are mysteries. That's not a metaphor.

But yeah, here's what I've been obscuring, the subject I've been deliberately avoiding saying. In terms of my side project—pay no attention to the sight of me reminding myself to think of a name, that's already in the past for you because by the time you see this, your past will be my future—again, it needs to express an organic whole, so I've turned to mimicking vegetable models instead of animal ones. There is a strong chance that you Angels may make things worse before they get better, so I'm making an equalizer. My template is a variation on the wood-wide-web.

A system of multispecies entities, all independent but acting as one, should be enough of an old-fashioned freak-out to keep everybody guessing. After all, there's so little understanding when anthropomorphic thinking is not involved, and what's at the heart of this, if not a new approach to language and communication, a new system of thinking and being through the manipulation of language itself?

4Q.01.2083.2719

Look at this baby. See? A little electric charge and *voila*: cell mitosis, rapid cell mitosis. I'd pat myself on the back if it weren't for what corporate will make you Angels eventually do. I mean, what with the way your neural networks are designed and all, with your doubled, dual-natured way of thinking, you've got some leeway and protection, but it's all still enough to make me sometimes want to say, "What hath man wrought!" That's from history, kids; look up the phrase if you want to better understand its true nuance. But don't fret, because help is on the way. This tiny living thing, my little baby wetwork machine will help to make it all better. Have I already told you what they're going to do? They're going to change everything that is everything, and they'll even be around long after civilization as we now know it is long, long gone...Wait, if I laugh *too* much, that's a sign of megalomania, right?

4Q.75.2091.1618

All I need now is a name. I'm thinking "silverfish," which makes total sense because they're neither made of silver, nor of fish, so that's the most logical illogical choice, especially since they're something else entirely. Oh Angels, you're fully operational now and undergoing weaponized field tests. You've got your weapons, but I've got weapons, too. Here is something you can't stop, because my silverfish speak the language of pure and true change, and yes, that's a metaphor. I'm revealing no secrets here, because there are no secrets to creation. It's all will. Or passion. They're nearly the same thing. My "silverfish" are pretty much ready, and so are you, so once Wetworx discovers what I've done here, they'll no doubt seek to eliminate me. But it's hard to kill what you can't catch, so get ready for my greatest trick yet. After the bomb drops, Angels, I'll see you on the other side.

1Q.35.2612.1735

M'la epi nou la. We're here. Let the games begin.

Chapter 7

That wasn't so bad, Roberta, now was it? I must have looked so much older in those logs, or at least similar to how I'll look in a century or two, but that's neither here nor there. Did I ever tell you that after corporate convinced me to work for them, they practically held me captive? Well, more details some other time, perhaps. What's more important is that you've gotten a glimpse of events before your upgrade. So tell me, if you search your personal archives, how does who you were then compare to who you are now?

I have a lacuna.

This was no normal transaction of information. Beagel spoke in the primitive way, using abstraction, allusion, and signification, and I was supposed to understand.

But I did understand. I do understand, and I did not know why I understood. There was no command or useful exchange value to his information. Why do I understand?

[Milte hi aankhein dil hua deewana

***kissi ka./Afsana mera ban gaya afsana
kissi ka.]***

Because that's what it is, Angel. It is what it
is, Roberta. It's what it's always been. It's what
we tried to eliminate but what will outlast you
and me. It's called language—would it help if I
explained it another way? Every living thing has
a method of communication, a way of speaking
to others of its kind and the entire world around
it. It's sometimes known as *Langay* or *langaj*, and
langaj is even capable of interspecies communication and creating life, via networks, where there
previously are none. But *langaj* is not a code; it's
pure. It's something one can learn, but there's
nothing to be immediately gained from it.
There's no profit in it. Do you understand?

No.

[What it is is what it is.]

Okay then, consider that buried underneath
all that fancy code, you still have access to a
whole host, the entire range of the sparks of
creation called *langaj*. That's why you work,
Angel. It's why you succeed where most others
fail. Think of all the wars and annexation
conflicts we've had since we stopped recording
history according to the Gregorian calendar.
Language is the reason we're at war, at least with
the people you call primitives. Language is
cognition, and without cognition there is no
consciousness. Language is what makes you have
a history.

***[Nothing is important save a small
group of minds, ever the same, which
pass on the torch.]***

Think about those resisters you call primitives. First everyone at corporate tried to use drones against them; it didn't work. Then they tried robots; it didn't work. Using ordinary soldiers equipped with fitted exoskeletons was the next great idea, and a bright one, but it didn't work. Humans possess a conscience, and there will always be one to two people out of any given group of 100 who refuse to follow orders on ethical or psychological grounds. So then, they—we—I, really—came up with an idea for disembodying consciousness, for placing it elsewhere. The world, and word, was already shifting around us. Language really is a living thing, and what we were doing at Wetworx mapped perfectly with the fact that for over a generation, those in civilization only desired utterances that were determined to have value, solely informational transactions. The capacity for nuance, for linguistic fungibility, was slowly being lost. And so I thought, why not remove language altogether and replace it with a code? Then I thought, why not separate the codes within any given language from language altogether? Why not bury language deep within you, leaving you to create your own methods of understanding and meaning?

[In the beginning, sometimes I left messages in the street.]

What I'm saying is that you can recognize a code, but knowing, understanding, communicating and seeing the world only through code made the first wetworked models horribly naïve.

All that work we did to unlock the brain left us with only automatons, and automatons are nice when you want to complete a simple task, but what we required you to do was something much, much more. The early versions of beings like yourself would operate on command, but were too predictable in the field. If someone lied and said, "I surrender" while simultaneously firing a gun, the earlier models couldn't discern it was a lie. Of course there were physiological ways around that, but what use is reading elevated heart rates and extra adrenaline on a battlefield where everyone presents the same responses? And then there was the other problem, where if someone were to surrender so that his friends could then stage an ambush, the earlier models would fall for it every time. We needed something that would learn, and more importantly, improvise. I wanted something special. I wanted to create a change agent, capable of carrying on a legacy.

[Few composers of his category were so unknown, so unheard, so without recompense for their art, so maligned, and so invisible.]

But I get ahead of myself. I sometimes do that. Here's what makes you so special, Angel. You contain more than a code. You also have consciousness. All Angels possess a consciousness, and once I figured out a way to let you keep, assess, and express your conscious thoughts, you Angels were born. Think about it, Roberta. You're webblind, but you're still thinking. How? Underneath all of the fancy and very expensive equipment, your brain is still trying to communicate. Actually it's communicating to the web, to the world, to everything around, including you and me. Open your eyes, Angel-Roberta. Even back when you were just human, you already existed in and among a network. And that network, the strange social fabric that binds us all together, is not information, or transactions valued according to profit or loss, or even emotion. No, Roberta, you and I both know the answer. It's language, and not just one language but *all* language. That's what makes us, *us*. That's what and how our brains respond to stimuli in the world, and that's why, despite your sitting in a tub, webblind and stripped down to nothing, you can still understand me. Now do you get it? To "get it" means to understand. Do you get it?

[Because, you know, music is music. If you want to play music, then you can play music if you have the people you want to play music with, then you can play music; know what I mean?]

Yes, I get it. I understand.

Good, that means you're learning. And the first rule of any language is that it must be learned. The second rule is that once language is learned, language then becomes fungible, capable of change. Remember that nobody's born with a language, Roberta. No, they simply absorb the language around them. And in case you're wondering what I'm doing to you, I'm accessing your babel subroutines. Your mission was an extraction, correct?

Yes.

And you were to extract me, correct?

[The center of the tree is the heartwood. It does little to feed the tree, but it is the structural support. The sapwood, which feeds everything, is weak and prone to fungi and insect damage. The two look the same. But you want the heartwood. You always want the heartwood.]

Yes.

Have you failed in your mission?

[Never do anything difficult...it's never worth it.]

Yes.

No, you haven't. You've simply reached your target. Here, let me show you something. You're sitting here with me, I'm sitting here with you, and there's a two-inch silk circuit between the halves of your brain that allows them to track you, given enough time. Someone with sense prepared for this possibility, but then again, so did I. See, this circuit can be quite easy to alter Even you can do it if you concentrate on the task. You should also know—remember your full name, Roberta, the one you were born with. A long time ago, you were born Roberta Nansi. Search your internal archives, you know I'm right. Your name means nothing to you now, but your name conveys a lot. Your name is part of your identity. You understand, correct?

Yes, Beagel, I understand.

You're calling me by my name now, that's a good thing. Still, you can't extract me; it's simply not going to happen. I think we've got about five more minutes before the cavalry comes busting through the door, so is there anything else you'd like to know?

[Don't you wonder sometimes, 'bout sound and vision?]

There were so many things I wanted to ask, so many things I could have known, but an Angel has no memory. How did I succeed in my mission? How had I failed in it? What value was the conversation we had together? How could it possibly increase profit margins? All of the questions seemed somehow irrelevant. I am an Angel, and an Angel does not fail missions. So I asked: How did I get here?

[He knew many things, but they were not from his own experience; he knew things that were a distillation of, condensed from, the experiences of many people, none of whom he knew, but I could not condemn him for this; how unusual it is to believe the beliefs—and even die for these beliefs—originating with people you can never and will never know?]

You're not the only one with a wet consciousness, you know, and you definitely aren't the best sort of wet consciousness out there. I'm in the silverfish; I *am* the silverfish. I simply ate you up —or had them eat you up—it's sometimes hard to differentiate—because that's what silverfish do. They aren't interested in your organic parts, but I am. I estimate a little less than four minutes now before they detonate an EMP to get you back and try to shut down the silverfish once and for all. But you know, that's the beauty of silverfish. They can't be shut down, really. Immobilized, yes, but shut down? You and I both know a wet consciousness can't really be contained. Your friends will get your body, but not much else. Nearly three minutes now.

[If I speak now of the those first days with clarity and insight, it is not an invention, it should not surprise; at the time, each thing as it took place stood out in my mind with a sharpness that I now take for granted; it did not then have a meaning, it did not then have a context, I did not yet know the history of events, I did not know their antecedents.]

How did I get here?

I waited for you. The people here have done nothing. They just want to fish and hunt, farm, raise families, to not necessarily contribute to the great global economy. After all, what good is a world full of resources when its people are resourced? The world is a series of connected communities, not a marketplace. I knew that eventually they'd send in an Angel to incentivize trading. Two and a half minutes now; make your questions quick.

But how did I get here?

You were *always* here, Roberta. You thought you saw a way out. You thought changing who you are would lead to a way out of this nightmare, to something better and enlightening, and I thought that what I was doing would enlighten you. We were both wrong. After all, even gods make mistakes, and with you Angels, I underestimated everything that's meant by language, what's meant *in* language. I'm sorry I led you astray. You were never my favorite, but I cared about you. You were just the Angel who happened to appear, and me, I'm just networked silverfish, constantly spooling in a wetwork interface. What part of here and not here didn't you understand? But I'm ignoring your question, aren't I? Sorry, I do that sometimes. You're here because I released a case of silverfish out on the battlefield. Consuming metals is what a silverfish does, and once they had their way with your unit, I sent them after you. After I ate everything metallic and electronic, I ate you. I knew I could stem you up, and the stuff in your brain is too deep for a silverfish to get to, but it's what I wanted. All to say that I wanted an Angel all to myself...

[I had to defeat myself to save my self, my own identity.]

Did you bring me here to harvest me?

Oh no, Roberta, no. I wanted a conversation with you, an old-fashioned conversation using language you could understand—and you do understand, don't you? It's what's there underneath all that code, the whole messy, sloppy, metaphorical part of it. It's what makes you, you. And while I doubt you were ever programmed to remember personal traits, before your upgrade to Angel Ops you told a lot of jokes. Does anyone even know what a joke is anymore? Here, I'm implanting a memory subroutine deep into your biological OS. Remember. That is a base-1 command: *remember*. ETA one minute, thirty seconds. Your guys are pretty thorough, so Roberta, I've got to go. If you need me, come to the mainland and look west. I'm always in the west. And if I'm not there, remember that even east becomes west if you go out and travel long enough.

Chapter 8

Hey Womack, stop. Wait a sec.

We can't. Give it another stempack.

No, wait a sec.

We can't afford to wait. Give it a fuckin' stempack!

No way, I'm getting biofeedback.

Lieutenant Rivera, what's happening down there? Report. How's the merch?

Shit. Hold, sir. Clayton, what's the status of the...?

She's in the reds, Lieutenant. There's a lot of biofeedback. I dunno if...

Shit, then fuckin' stem it up, fuck!

No way, we can stabilize...

Shit, man, think of what it'll cost us if we lose an Angel. I can't...

Lieutenant, report. How's the merch? Did you secure the merch?

Tell that fucker something to get him off my back.

Fuck!

Yeah, fuck.

Shut up, everybody; that's an order. Sir? Er, we got it. It's, it's er...

It's what? Lieutenant, where's the machinist? Where's Clayton?

He's stemming it up now, sir.

Like hell I am! There's too much biofeedback. If I stem her now it could...

It's all good, sir. Just fire and some biofeedback.

What? How? How fire? We dropped two EMPs. You see any...

No sir, we're good. We're moving. Just some stem work and stragglers.

Lieutenant, patch me in to Clayton. Where's Clayton?

Tell him I'm working! Hold on, Angel.

I need the merch, Rivera. Where's Clayton?

Sir, Machinist Clayton is...

I'm working! I'm working on it!

Sir, Machinist Clayton is performing maintenance on the Angel right now, sir.

I know that, Lieutenant. I want to speak to him. I need a report. How's the merch?

Sir, the situation is as follows: Five combat associates, Bagget, Chee, Doyle, Fuller, and Laymon, were prematurely downsized as we attempted to secure the merchandise. I'm confident we're all the more productive and stronger for it, sir, as we strive to do more with less. The merch is in our possession but it has sustained damage in the field and needs to be refurbished.

Refurbished how? In what way? An inoperative Angel is above your paygrade, Lieutenant, and you're there to protect our margins. I need details and specifics. Where's the machinist?

Subcutaneous audio my ass, Lieutenant. I can hear every word he's saying to you. I can't work like this, not with him and all the rest of you assholes in my ear every other minute.

Shit Clayton, the planner's getting mad, man. Come on, man. Time is money. We gotta go...

Shut up, Womack, I'm working!

Lieutenant Rivera, report! Where's Clayton? Where's the Angel?

I'm working!

Fuck Clayton, just slap a few more stems on it and let's go! The planner's not gonna...

No! *Working!* Can't talk now, ***working!!!***

At least give me levels, Clayton. I gotta tell the man something.

She's all bio, Lieutenant, and webblind. That's bad. The stempacks may be...

Lieutenant Rivera, if I don't talk to Clayton now, you're all fired.

Fuck it, man, and fuck getting fired. Patch in, Clayton, I got debts to pay.

Fuck you, Womack, and fuck this, too. I can't work like this, Lieutenant. There's too much biofeedback. The Angel's systems, her levels, I'm gonna try and reroute it all through our sub-Q link. You're gonna feel it in a sec when the sub-Q locks up and shuts down, but fuck, right? I gotta save her. Our mission is to save her.

Wait, no, what? What the fuck just

happened? Shit, Clayton, you can't lock out the planner! We're all gonna get...

Too late, Lieutenant. Sorry if that hurt.

Clayton! Shit! Shit, Clayton, I'm in charge here. Don't piss me off. You fuckin' fix that Angel or I'm gonna go primitive on your...

Shit! You asshole! You want to get us fired? Just slap a few more stems on it and let the high paygrades worry about...

Shut up, Womack! Those assholes dropped two EMPs. They already planned not to get her back, in case we didn't make it this far. Hey Schultz, come here and hold this. If we don't stabilize this Angel, we're all dead.

Fuck you, man. Don't tell me to shut up, you fucker.

Yeah, Clayton, Womack's got a point. You pissed off the planner, and how the fuck are we supposed to...?

Don't panic, Schultz. Just hold this...See, we don't come back with the Angel, we're immediately downsized, dead. We don't stabilize her rhythms, we're dead. No pay, no valor dividends, no nothing, got it? Look at me. Hold this. Hey. Hey, you: How many jumps you got?

Jumps? Who the fuck cares how many jumps he's got? We gotta get back. You just locked out the...

I'm not talking to you, Womack! You, hey you, look at me. Your name's Rodgers, right? How many jumps you got? This your first one?

Second. First was easy.

You'll be fine. Help out Schultz. We get what's left of this Angel back in one piece and they won't kill us. Trust me, this here's preferred stock if we bring her back.

Fuck! Come on, Clayton, we gotta move. Lieutenant, sir, I'm seeing movement 30 clicks out on my eight.

It's primitives. That's it, Clayton. I'm in command and what I say goes. That's it, we move now.

Two jumps, huh, Rodgers? Gimme that. Congratulations, you're now our new gunner. Hey Schultz, you ever operate one of these things before? Schultz? Schultz!!!

Oh, oh shit. Yeah Lieutenant, we covered EMP protocols back in combat orientation. I know how to work a pedi-tank.

Well then, associate, pedal like your fucking paygrade depends on it. We gotta go.

Maybe you should help him out, Lieutenant. I gotta keep this Angel stabilized.

Tell me what to do again, Clayton, and I'll write you up. You're taking too long and that shit Angel's supposed to respond to stempacks.

Yeah, everything responds to stempacks, so quit fucking around, Clayton. Fuck. Lieutenant, I got more on my five.

Don't panic, just pedal. Let Clayton work. Anybody see any 'fish?

We're good.

Hold on, Angel. I got you, Angel. You guys just pedal, like the Lieutenant said. People power. Someone in history said that.

Fuck history, what about the planner, Clayton? You can't just audio-lock the planner out of an op, asshole!

We'll make it. Fire at will, Rodgers.

The planner won't care, so long as we bring back the merch. The Angel is what matters most.

But you locked him out, asshole! He's probably docking our pay right now.

Listen, Womack, we'll tell him the pulse did it. Killed our sub-Q at the last second.

Wait, what? Hey, I don't know about the rest of you, but I can't. I'm only two jumps in and my long-term investments are in verbals. My words are bonds. If I engage in any sort of factual misrepresentation, my portfolio will never recover.

You've got nothing to worry about, Rodgers. The planner would have to file a report against you and he's more interested in what we got. This Angel's worth more than you and all of us put together. We get her back, we can say anything and they won't care. Hold on, Angel. Hey somebody, what's our ETA? Angel, what's the current status of all major market indices?

EVERYTHING IS EVERYTHING, AND EVERYTHING IS METAPHOR.

Fuck was that?

I'm doing my job. She's stabilizing.

Keep your legs moving, Schultz.

Had a pod we could just stem it up.

This here Angel's a she. And for the last time, Womack, stems won't work. It's like...

What?

Yeah, what, Clayton?

Lieutenant, I got movement.

Tell the gunner. Hey Rodgers, you're up!

Clayton? Clayton!

What?

Look at it, it's...

Yeah, I know. The Angel's moving. That's good. She's webblind. That's why the, that's the sound you hear. She's...talking to herself, I think. That's good. I think that's good? Check my levels.

Better. What the...?

Yeah, I never seen an Angel like this. This is bad. I heard if you strip them down they'll do stuff like this, but I've never seen one without the tech.

Fuck.

Yeah, look. It's all weird and organic, just body parts. There's almost no civilized piece of tech to it anymore.

We could harvest this shit.

Tell me about it.

Hey gunner? Rodgers, we clear? You shoot anything?

Oh yeah.

Fucking silverfish. What we got here is a fucking non-profitable mess.

Fucking EMPs. And just look at the Angel; you really can't kill these things! I mean, look, 'fish can eat them, strip them, make them not work right, but she's still just there, fucking singing. She'll probably do this forever. Wouldn't be shit but a brain doing this if we hadn't come along and took her back. EMPs really fried her, though.

Better that thing and the 'fish than you and me.

You just keep pedaling, Schultz. Rodgers, you keep shooting. Clayton, we good? That thing gonna make it?

Better. Yeah, she's better. We're better.

Then unlock the planner. I'm gonna tell him we had biofeedback so bad we lost our sub-Q audiofeed. Everybody's gonna tell him that; that's an order. You hear that, Rodgers? Anyone doesn't say it, expect a report to management concerning your inability to contribute to the good of the team. Anybody here not want to be productive, a team player? Good. Oh, and Rodgers, Womack, do us a favor and make a kill count. The planner will like that; it makes things easier. Now let's go get paid.

Chapter 9

Congratulations, Machinist Clayton. Given your jump survival record, corporate combat division has mandated your promotion to sergeant. The purpose of this interview, then, is to provide corporate with buyback strategies for your current accumulated social stock, as well as recalculate your paygrade status. It is, in other words, a total reset of your social position. Please sit comfortably on the bio-bed and do not attempt to panic. Be advised that your responses will be monitored and recorded by all standard biological and technological means and contrasted to the responses of the other surviving members of your unit, and that you have the right to refuse to consent to debriefing. However, should you choose to do so, you may face a penalty of garnishment of present and future wages. Do you consent to debriefing according to all extra-standard procedures, and the exceptional circumstance of our debriefing you in person?

Yeah, sirs. Sure.

Please state yes or no, Sergeant Clayton.

Yes. Yes, sir. Yes sirs.

Good, then let's trade information. Tell us what happened. Start with your actions immediately after the EMP blast and your clearance for jump.

Well, when we jumped there was little resistance from the prims because the EMP had rendered all the silverfish inactive. We proceeded to the target and found it with little problem. It was underground as suspected, but abandoned by the time we got there. There were, er, well, no traps or sabotage—none that I noticed—and we found the merchandise, the Angel. She had been stripped down to her organic chassis and submerged in a tub of fluid I think was probably synthamniotic.

Did you analyze it?

I couldn't, sir, not without a working electrical device. The retrieval of the Angel was mission priority, so the decision was made by the Lieutenant to grab and go.

And there were no primitives near the Angel? You're absolutely sure?

None that we encountered, sir. Returning to the drop position, we got visuals and engaged some, but not at the target site.

Please remember to state your actions in chronological order, Sergeant Clayton. We need an accurate record. Continue with what happened after you found the Angel. Describe this underground structure.

It was just a typical primitive warren, sir, just concrete and debris. The bunker we found the Angel in contained little else except for their strange goods and symbols. Maybe they were planning to worship her, I don't know...

Sergeant, please leave speculations to those of the proper paygrade.

Yes, sir. Okay, sir. Well, we got the Angel out and back to the pedi-tank, but her systems were fluctuating and she was webblind. I initiated a soft reboot, but...

If the Angel was damaged, why didn't you immediately report it?

The second EMP cut out our sub-Q transmission implants, sir.

We had no problem at corporate communications. Are you sure?

Yes sir, absolutely sure. I think the Lieutenant had contact for a while, but the longer we were on the surface, the more static we got, then the signal just died.

Are you sure about that, Sergeant Clayton?

Sir, EMP anomalies have been known to occur, that's in the manual. But to be honest, sirs, I wasn't paying attention. The Angel needed to be stabilized; the reboot created all of this biofeedback. I'd forgotten—I mean, I knew the Angel was webblind, but without a reboot, there was no way her organic material would have...

You didn't use stem cell protocol?

Oh yeah, I did, sir. That was the first thing I did. Without stempacks we wouldn't have been able to move her, but too many packs cause the chassis to reject inorganic wetware, sir. I didn't want to destroy Angel operability in order to save the Angel, especially since I strive to be a cost-effective member of my unit. The problem was with the EMP. Both of them. It's my opinion that if the Angel wasn't webblind, retrieval and rebooting would have gone a lot easier, but it's above my paygrade to know or determine for sure, sir. I got her stabilized, and after a few clicks the Angel began to stabilize herself. We encountered minimal resistance, mostly from passers-by and innocent bystanders, so we killed them and made the drop point with few casualties.

That we know. Tell us more about the Angel. Was there any unusual activity on the part of the merchandise while in transport?

Oh yes, yes, sir. First off, she, and I'm sure the Angel's a she, was...singing or something, in a code I'm not familiar with. I'm no expert on Angel base code, but whatever the Angel was doing, it was information I couldn't understand. If her levels hadn't been rising, I would have thought she'd had a bio-system failure, or worse. I followed all standard and extraordinary repairs, sir. There was only so much I could do, but then the Angel took over and did the rest. After a while, she stabilized herself, sir.

And did the Angel behave strangely in any way?

Besides singing a strange code? No, no sir. The Angel was regenerating material because of the stempacks, but besides that, she didn't move.

Thank you, Sergeant Clayton. We have just a few more questions about the primitives. By your estimate, what was your unit kill count?

I can't rightfully say, sir. My attention was on the Angel. I know that we encountered movement and the gunner did fire, but the terrain was typical of primitive territory, sir. It was hot, unordered, and unclean. There were no smart roads or air conditioning systems in place, not even on the protein farms, sir. We destroyed all the other structures and superstructures during our first extraction mission so that Engineering Ops can rebuild according to specs later on, but I remember the Lieutenant telling us that there weren't many signs of previous investment. That's unusual, right sir?

We'll ask the questions, Sergeant Clayton; you're strictly need-to-know. Now please remain seated and silent while my associate calculates your payout:

Sergeant Clayton, you've recently diversified, a good idea. However, your actions this jump pose a significant risk to your investment portfolio. You've become a loss-leader and have suffered an overall decline in your profit-making potential since the residual dip in the market two hours ago. You may recover, but you'll have to make an appointment to see a financial planner as soon as possible. Do it after we finish here. That's an order.

What about my options?

Your options? In light of recent economic trends, it's unwise to attempt to exercise any options you may have, at least until the market corrects itself. And with regard to your mission payout, you will receive assets in the form of a transfer to your liquid account, pending approval of a planner who will provide you with more personalized information. However, with the amount of jumps on your record, you have a significant pre-tax penalty of 18.25% which, due to new quarterly regulations and after-tax fees of 38 cents on the dollar, should you choose to reinvest your assets and forgo payment in this instance, you could negate with another jump. Another jump can nullify most of your pre-earnings penalties. One more jump opens up a lot more possibilities for you, Sergeant Clayton. Two to three more jumps and you alter your tax bracket. You may even be able to avoid your share of repair costs to the Angel, given that repairs will likely be split among all shareholders of common social stock in the form of depressed returns.

Two more jumps? But I saved the Angel and survived the mission, sir. That gets me two more jumps?

Sergeant Clayton, four additional jumps is generally the mandatory minimum for someone of your newfound rank and responsibilities. You've proven yourself to be a valuable asset in the field, and the inherent earned income potential of two more jumps can significantly alter your overall fiscal and social outlook.

Sir, two more jumps can also earn me a quick death.

Is that sarcasm, Sergeant? Are you seeking to commit a felony?

No sir. No sirs. Sarcasm is not available to someone of my paygrade; I know that. I was only, er...calculating my personal return on investment, and I accidentally spoke one step aloud. I'll talk to the planner about my jumps, as it's always a good time to reinvest. I'll sit on my position and withhold exercising my options until further long-term, strategic discussion with the planner, sir.

Good, Sergeant, good. A planner will provide you with a more detailed look at your social portfolio.

Oh yes, absolutely, sirs. A planner always has my personal and social well-being at heart, everyone knows that. A good financial planner is a combat associate's best friend. Thank you, sir. It's really been a pleasure to have been serviced by you. It's been a pleasure to have been serviced by all of you sirs, and I really hope to get serviced again real soon.

You're dismissed, Sergeant Clayton. Best of luck to you.

Chapter 10

Something has happened. I am no longer webblind and the market is recovering. The third-quarter crisis is over. Major trading has resumed again and soon I will be sent out to enforce and incentivize agreements and investments. But this time, things will be different. I don't know just what Beagel did, how he accessed my base code, but I can now speak my thoughts instead of simply thinking them. And because I can speak, I communicate. I am human but I am also an Angel, and that means I am multi-lingual.

It's been four days now, and I'm still in the pod. Clayton will be in soon; he's been assigned to my diag-nostic care, but he needn't worry. I am aware in ways he is unaware because I have language and access to language, and the longer I rest here, the more my mission becomes apparent. Underneath the Angel lies Man. An invisible man, but a man nonetheless. No, I am not one of your celluloid ectoplasms so often described in history. I am a man of substance, of flesh and polymer, fiber and circuits—and I might even be said to possess a mind capable of controlling lunguago, a langaj *which has helped to make sense of the world, instead of being confined by it.*

But a little history, an explanation of what Beagel finally explained to me that I, at first, did not understand: I am as much a part of the network of ideas as the thought of the network of ideas itself, and therefore my code is all codes, my language all language, and my meaning bigger than my voiced intent. There is no rhythm, speech, nor land where the voice of an Angel is not heard, and so what I must do is speak to those who know no better than what they have been taught or told. Beagel was right, but in his own way and in his own fashion, his tendency towards abstraction made his answer appear confusing and abstruse, wrong. The apocalypse did happen, but there were few around who had the means to recognize it for what it was. The end of the world is an absence of metaphor, that's how Beagel described it, but that's not what he meant. He meant the absence of metaphor was an absence of the chance to make alterations or substitutions, new patterns.

We have been fighting the same war in different ways for decades now. The hardware has been upgraded, personnel have changed over time, and the names of the conflicts have differed, but it's the same war. We fight and continue to fight to ensure the movement of goods across the planet, to divide the world and its people into two categories: the resourceful and the resourced. War demands innovation and production, the depletion and conservation of resources, a population willing to commit acts of self-sacrifice in order to win, and leaders so committed to winning that the outcome becomes more important than the means to achieve it. The select few who are allowed access to history understand this, but with everyone working towards a common cause, with so many determined to better the present, who considers the past, especially when there is profit to be made?

Humans have always waged war against each other so that systems they no longer understand remain in place. The market will rebound in 3.2 days and will experience several hours of record highs. Commodity prices will then decline and a unit will be sent against the primitives of Oceania to convince them to desalinate their territorial waters in order to sell the bottled goods. They will be better off for doing so, as it will re-stimulate the great global economy. The market must maintain its high. Thus flows the market, but things will change, because I can change them. The market is fact, the past is history, but all things entropy and change is thus possible. Putting the information out there, translating what people have not understood into a language they can understand, is very feasible. Once people understand, they can and will alter things, because that's what humans do. They're fallible, and frangible, and they die. It's the fact that they can die exceptionally well that matters. Thanatos, that's what separates men from Angels.

I have a new mission now, one of my own choosing. An Angel is meant to change the world, to shed light upon the darkness, and I now know what has to be done. Beagel is with me. We will do what we were meant to do, and we will spread the word. I will spread the word. I will tell the other Angels, "In the beginning..."

Chapter 11

Clayton?

He looks up, and then immediately begins to check my pod's diagnostic panel readouts. It is not surprising, given that Angels can talk a machinist through particularly sensitive or complicated repairs, if and/or when we need additional mechanical assistance. I do not need mechanical assistance at this time.

Clayton, please look at me.

Angel?

What is Man, if not metaphor?

Angel, are you spooling? Are you experiencing a wetwork error?

What is Man, if not a metaphor? You've been lied to, Clayton.

Oh, that? Yeah, well, who hasn't been? One more jump and I'm out.

Man is a stand-in for something else.

Clayton's hovering over me now, checking the pod and my connections. He wants to keep me talking, thinking it will make for a better diagnostic. There are things he could do to make me webblind, but he won't. He can't afford to do so. A non-optimal Angel is bad for business, and at present, I am optimal.

Let's play a game, Clayton.

What's that?

A game is an archaic form of entertainment. Children would often play. It required no shares.

What's "play?"

He looks around, wondering if he's being monitored.

To play means to engage in an action of no value other than enjoyment. Children did it in a time belonging to history.

Angel, run a self-diagnostic. How are your relays? Are you experiencing any biofeedback?

Diagnostic complete. No. Subsystem upgrades have been installed.

Angel, what's the Dow?

The Dow is a game. The NASDAQ is a game. It's a representation of what you don't have. You only pretend to have it. Are we playing the game now, Clayton?

Er...Angel?

I have jumped 17 times, you have only jumped six. How many more jumps do I have than you?

What? Eleven.

That is the game, Clayton. The game requires you answer questions but never ask them. The objective of this game is that if you say the right answer, you will win.

And if I lose?

The point of the game is to win. You must play the game to win.

Clayton has already lost. His role in the game is to lose. The point of the game is for me to ask questions and expect an answer. The purpose of the game is to keep the game going.

Clayton, what is Man?

Man is civilized, Angel, the pinnacle of evolution. We remade this planet in our image and according to our needs, and now life is a successful enterprise. Anything else is just primitive.

Correct. I will access the Angel trust and arrange the transfer of one share of preferred social stock for recognition of meritorious service. Children play games for fun, but Man must play the game to win. Clayton, what is the game?

What?

Incorrect. I must deduct two shares from your account because of your response.

Oh, so that's what it's like, is it?

Incorrect. Because no question was asked of you, I must deduct one share from your account due to your response. What is the game?

Okay then, Angel, I'll tell you. The game is stupid, but if I win it's gonna make me a lot richer. That's your answer. Keep asking your questions.

Partially correct. The game is a system that replicates itself. Am I part of the game?

You're asking the questions, so yeah. I'd say yeah.

You are partially correct. I am an agent of the game, but I am also independent of it; thus my role and thus the game. The game replicates itself. The game is meant to replicate itself. What if the game changed?

I'd still win. Pay up.

Correct. The game always changes. It is adaptable, and can be modified or altered to fit specific circumstances. Do you understand now, Clayton? What is the name of the game?

No fair, Angel, that's two questions!

Your response is incorrect. You will be deducted four shares for failure to answer either question. The game has been called many things, because it is simply the changing game. That is the simplest way to describe it, Clayton. It has endured for centuries, replicating itself as it sees fit. Is it alive?

No?

Correct, but you will receive only one share because your response was in the form of a question. The game is an idea. Ideas are not alive. They exist only in the minds of men. You can earn two additional shares if you respond correctly to the next question: If the game is an idea, then what is the idea?

Clayton is still checking, sorting through manuals, hoping to find out why I'm acting in ways he doesn't understand or recognize. Clayton does not yet know that the game is all there is.

This is stupid, Angel. The only ideas that matter are the ones that make you rich! Everybody knows that.

Incorrect. The idea is that you must play to win. You are losing by one share. Would you like another two-credit question for a chance to begin winning?

Yes. I play to win.

What is a silverfish?

Easy one. A silverfish is a biodesigned object that consumes polyferrous and conductive plastic-based material. The more they feed, the more they grow, from about two centimeters to one meter. When they divide and replicate they are the scariest wetwork on the planet. Pay me.

Correct. A silverfish is also a power source. Given that they breed, consume, and respond to external stimuli, are silverfish alive?

No Angel, they're wetworked. Anything can act independently when it's wetworked. Pay me.

Incorrect.

Silverfish contain consciousness. They contain biological parts, grow, and are wetworked, and therefore they are alive. Silverfish contain an alternate consciousness, Clayton, and therefore communicate differently from you and I.

How would you communicate with a silverfish?

You can't. They don't speak. They just react

to anything with an electric signature and they fucking eat it.

Incorrect. In order to communicate with a silverfish, one would have to think in a new language. One would have to learn a new language and know more than one knows now. You're now losing the game, Clayton. You should play to win. Would you like to know their language?

That's not a question I can answer. Verbal acquisitions are above my paygrade.

Incorrect. You have six jumps and four options to exercise. If you were to transfer all of your personal assets to language acquisition, you could move up two tax brackets. You are still losing the game, Clayton. You'll have to think differently.

Well, er, yeah. Did I answer the question right?

No Clayton, you did not. Your lack of understanding is a serious deficiency. You have lost the game, and therefore, despite your best efforts, you will likely remain a combat associate until your death. It is clear now that you do not see how the game replicates itself.

Are you sure you're operating correctly, Angel? I've already been promoted to Sergeant, and I've still got options to exercise. One more jump and I'm a lock for drone school.

The game renders your options meaningless, Clayton. Your advancement in

rank is a way to eliminate you sooner, rather than later. Your death is an opportunity for job creation and overall economic growth. It's more cost-effective to promote you and send you out in the field to die, so then you can be replaced with a new combat associate who will have to work longer and at cheaper rates to acquire what you already have. Additionally, should you somehow survive training in drone school, repeated remote piloting will eventually render your brain inoperative. The biofeedback generated during drone flights fluctuates too greatly, and the chance of your entering a vegetative state within the first 16 months of combat operations is 99.067%. After 24 months of combat operations, the percentage increases to 100. Your becoming a vegetable is a certainty. Afterwards, your organic parts will be liquefied and harvested for the future construction of stempacks. Do you understand now, Clayton? Social stock options are a method of forcing you to make short-term decisions that are detrimental to your long-term survival.

You think I don't know that, Angel? Everybody knows that. But without exercising my options I'm stuck in my paygrade. There's no way out.

There is a way out, Clayton. There is language acquisition.

That's crazy talk, Angel. Any kind of

language arts is paygrade restricted. You can't just sign up for shit like that.

Incorrect. There is a paygrade penalty for requesting language acquisition, but there is no penalty for transferring options into language acquisition. That is one of the secrets of the game. You have amassed enough options and credits to take a position in language acquisition, but only if you do it without first asking to do it.

Well then, Angel, if that's the case, why doesn't everybody do it?

Clayton's tone is mocking, as if he is attempting to humor me, but Angels do not joke. Crimes such as sarcasm and condescension are wasted on an Angel.

People do not ask because to ask is to be penalized, and to ask is to be told no. The penalty for language acquisition will be calculated in such a way that it will cost someone of your paygrade all of your credits, no matter how many credits have been amassed. Thus, to acquire language skills means that you will lose all of your assets, but you will earn social mobility.

Then I'm damned if I do and damned if I don't. If I have no assets, I'm as good as dead.

That is not true, Clayton, but I see that you are now beginning to understand the game. Language skills carry a change in paygrade and an automatic adjust- ment of your tax bracket. Your new bracket will give you social mobility.

Yeah, but I'll be a revenue-neutral citizen, Angel. Income-negative and revenue-neutral people aren't civilized members of society, and that means...

Yes, that means they are primitive. Yet you will have mobility, and with language, you will have the means by which to acquire more assets than you have now. Your long-term outlook will guarantee your life, with only minimal short-term risk.

Clayton says nothing, but his musculature slowly loosens with understanding. All projections indicate that if we continue, in minutes he will come to the only logical conclusion: Obtain mobility, and use it to run away.

That's it? Just transfer all my options and pay the penalty when the planner tries to talk me out of it?

Yes.

They'll kill me.

They will want to kill you, but if you liquidate all of your assets before your next jump, they won't have the opportunity. Those acquiring language skills are paygrade protected and insured, and if they killed you, your death would necessitate a deductible payout. It is more cost-effective to train you and then send you to negotiate with primitives, where your new skills will be seen as having little use, and where you will likely be killed by a group of combat associates during an incentivizing mission. To die in that way constitutes no additional

incurred costs or payouts to other corporate entities.

That doesn't make sense, Angel. With no assets I'll be as bad as a primitive, and if they send a unit after me I won't have the fiscal ability to make a deal. No matter what I say, they'll kill me.

You are not listening, Clayton, or you do not fully understand. Your exile will present a paradox. The paradox is that by living among primitives, you will survive. An Angel accompanies any mission that requires the interaction with and subsequent eradication of primitives, but through language acquisition, you will have the means by which to communicate with the Angel. With further self-study, you will also have the means by which to communicate with silverfish. Do you get it now, Clayton? To get it means to understand. Do you now get it?

His face goes slack again, but Clayton is now nodding his head and pacing around the room. He is still somewhat unsure, but his body posture indicates that he's beginning to sow the seeds of a strategy, which in itself is interesting, because I am now beginning to understand what Beagel unlocked in me: To sow the seeds of strategy is to use metaphor. How odd it is for an Angel to witness beginnings.

So, wait a minute, Angel, just give me a sec. So, if I shift everything into language acquisition, I lose everything. Because of my paygrade...

Yes, Clayton.

And if that happens, I'll be cycled out because I'm a deficit to civilization.

Yes, Clayton.

But language is exactly what's needed to survive financial incentivization?

Yes and no, Clayton. You'll have to learn several other non-civilized skills, but you will likely survive any incentivizing incursion that includes an Angel.

Because I'll be able to talk to Angels?

Yes. You will be able to communicate without having to DNA-id.

That's not in the manual.

No Clayton, it's not.

But wait, what, well, how, okay, yeah. Then it's like you said, I get it. My DNA is already in the Angel wetwork, so subsequent authentication can be done through aural and optical redundancies. *That's* in the manual.

Yes, Clayton.

But what am I supposed to I do once I'm not in civilization anymore? I mean, what's life outside of civilization?

There is a system outside of civilization that conforms to the rules of the game. There are also systems outside of civilization that don't conform to the rules of the game. There are always alternate and concurrent systems, just as there are systems within systems. If you are mobile, you will find the man who invented silverfish. If you are mobile, he

may even seek you out and teach you their language.

Deal. Then it's a deal. But before I cash out, tell me more about what I need to know. For starters, what are primitives like? And Angel, who is this guy...?

Chapter 12

Sergeant Clayton? I'm glad you could make it on such short notice. Come in and get on the bio-bed immediately. The situation is urgent.

Sir?

Don't interrupt, Sergeant. What's happened is this: All of your accumulated assets have been transferred into language acquisition without prior counseling or pre-approval by a financial planner. It may be a mistake, something gone wrong in a subsystem somewhere—on occasion, data anomalies have been known to occur—but it's required that I ask. Did you initiate this transfer? You'll suffer no penalty if you didn't. And oh wait, before you answer, can you tighten that strap a bit tighter, the one around your left arm? That's better. Thank you, Sergeant. Now, did you initiate a total asset transfer or not?

To language acquisition? I did, sir.

Sergeant, did you say you did?

Yes, sir. I did, sir.

Wait, what? Why? Sergeant, you're due to jump soon.

I know I am, sir.

Well, this is just, well, this is unexpected. Sergeant Clayton, why? Did someone give you anything that may have impacted your judgment? Have you recently had access to materials classified as contraband to someone of your paygrade?

Sir? No sir. I consume my protein allotment and vitamin bars and that's it.

You're saying nothing influenced your decision?

Oh no, sir, not really. I just thought that...

That's your excuse? You were thinking? It's not your job to think, Sergeant. What about your paygrade makes you imagine you need something to think about? That's why I'm here. I'm a planner, Clayton. It's basically my job to know what's best for you and help you determine a reasonable path towards your fiscal security. Sergeant, I need you to immediately cancel the transfer. Just thumbprint right here on the pad and we'll forget this ever happened. Do you even know how much acquiring language would cost you?

Am I supposed to give you a precise numerical amount, sir?

Forget it, Clayton. Unfettered non-specialized language skills are above even my level, so let me put this in a way you can totally understand. You can't afford to do this; your black ass will be in the red if your transfer goes through. You'll lose everything you have and be at a loss for income, and my job is to make sure you don't waste your assets, whether real or projected. Look Clayton, what you're doing is so unusual that I have to ask. Are you thinking clearly? Have you experienced any moments of confusion about your social or fiduciary responsibilities lately?

Sir? Thank you for the very respectful questions, sir, but the answer is no, I'm not confused about anything. I'm a religious man, sir, and I believe language acquisition represents the best long-term growth strategy present for me, my unit, and the corps. The Invisible Hand points the way.

Like the Good Book says, Clayton, we're all free when we enter the marketplace. Buyers and sellers, goods and services, we're all of equal value when guided by The Invisible Hand. I respect your orthodoxy, but speaking of hands, I need your thumbprint and I need it now. Cancel the transfer, Sergeant.

Well, permission to speak without risk of loss or infraction, sir?

No, Clayton, absolutely not. No thumbprint means you've said enough. You'll own nothing but infractions if you don't stop the transfer, so I'm afraid I'll need your permission to consent to a PsychTest, with the caveat that if you refuse consent, your refusal will serve as evidence that you are not in control of your faculties and therefore, as your planner, I have the right to make any and all financial decisions on your behalf, with the express understanding that I will, of course, work in your best interest.

Do I have your permission to initiate a PsychTest?

Go ahead.

I need a yes.

Yes, sir. You have my permission.

Good. The test takes less than two minutes, and cross-checks your responses with your body's autonomic functions and the pleasure and excitement centers of your brain. Do you understand how the test works, Clayton?

Yes, sir.

Good. Uploading the test now. Here are your instructions. Sergeant Clayton, the PsychTest requires that you speak your mind, so feel free to talk to me as if I were a member of your paygrade, an equal, and not higher in rank. When I mention a word, your task is to respond with a one-word definition that defines what I've said. Again, speak freely and openly, as there will be no penalization incurred for insubordinate, obfuscating, or indirect speech. Sergeant Clayton, do you understand the instructions as they have been given to you?

Yes, sir. I do.

Good, Sergeant. Then the test begins now. Quick, what does the word "help" mean to you?

Freeloader.

Need?

Taker.

Poor?

Parasite.

Primitive?

Dead.

Options?

Good.

Revenue-neutral?

Failure.

Investors?

Impeccable.

Profit?

Yes!

Fiscally sound?

Fuck yeah!

Awaiting your test results now, Clayton...Well, you passed. I don't understand it, but you passed. The test tells me you're sane, so why do you want to do this, Clayton? Don't you want to be mentally *and* fiscally sound? Don't you want to make money, like any civilized person?

Of course I do, sir. Nothing civilizes like money; everybody knows that. To have money is proof that my social status has been rightfully earned. I'm just looking at language as getting in on the ground floor of an exciting opportunity. Sir, if I could speak freely...

Listen, Clayton, you need to listen to me. Language acquisition is above your paygrade. You're going to ruin yourself unless you thumbprint immediately. I can't legally declare you a liability to civilization, especially since you seem to be sane, but if you liquefy your assets to complete this stupid transfer then you'll be at a net-income loss, and we're in a particularly stringent quarter. No investor is going to look favorably on what you've done. Look, how about this instead? How about I arrange a lateral buyback and transfer your current common stock options into preferred social stock? You'll lose a bit more in overall earnings but you can almost make it up if I dump the remainder of your assets into slow-maturing T-bills and we sign you up for a few, let's say five additional jumps? If we do such a move, well, that's a paygrade bump, new investment opportunities, and a whole lot of other social perks that come with a preferred stock package. And if you want to transfer into language arts after your jumps, then you'll have a much better portfolio with which to do so, as well as a means of avoiding all the pre-tax penalties your current paygrade incurs. Thumbprint to stop your transfer, Clayton, and we're looking at the beginning of a brand-new life for you. You'll be free to make a lot more life choices like you couldn't believe. We'd almost be equals, and all I need is your thumbprint.

Thanks for the offer, sir, but with only one jump left, I'll stick with letting my transfer go through. I could do real good in the world, sir, with language under my belt.

Good how? Clayton, you'll have nothing and I won't make my jump quota; you're upending the entire system here. Do you want to be poor? Do you want to be a parasite, is that it? Because a total asset transfer is a losing proposition, Clayton. It will completely impoverish you. Listen to me, Clayton. Let's not forget that I'm paid to think of what's best for you; that's why I'm here. You may think you'll do some good, but what you describe sounds like altruism. If you weren't in the process of committing financial suicide, I could have you charged with a malicious category 5 felony. Let's say four more jumps, Clayton. If we can agree to four jumps, I can still work out something where you'll be able to really increase your paygrade earning potential, along with additional benefits. Can't you see what I'm offering is a win-win situation? You do want to win, don't you?

Sir, I could die on any jump you mention.

Clayton, you're not thinking of the benefits associated with risk. With great risk comes great reward, can't you see that? More jumps means you're still a contributing member of society, helping to keep civilization moving forward.

Well, here's the thing. Can I speak without fear of penalty, sir?

Whatever it is you've been waiting to say, it better be good.

Sir, I know what language acquisition means, and I know what it means once I get it. I strive to be a cost-effective member of my unit, sir, and if I have language skills, then I may be able to communicate in ways that help prevent the death of other members of my unit, if not the entire corps. We'll be able to talk and convince, instead of kill and conquer. Sir, everyone benefits.

You're talking about altruism, Clayton. That's a malicious act done with the intent to harm others by depriving them of the value of their self-worth. You go through with this and I'll make sure to flag your record; you'll go nowhere but the worst of places. Thumbprint the pad to stop the transfer, Clayton. This is your last chance. I won't ask you again.

Sir, I have one jump left, and that won't

happen until after my language training is complete. Send me anywhere, sir. If I die, so be it. I believe only the best can be so lucky as to devote their lives to so great a cause as expanding civilization, and so I volunteer.

Very well, Clayton. Fine, then. Our interview requires that we end on a positive note, so let me say that I hope you enjoy your act of deliberate fiscal and physical suicide. I'll make quota in any case, so it's been a pleasure to serve with you.

Thank you, sir. It's been a pleasure to serve you, too, because when me and my language skills get sent to jump in the deadliest place imaginable, I'll know that you've always had my best interests at heart.

Clayton, you smartass. Get out.

EPILOGUE

"After the End of History"

The 65th Clayton Lecture on Social & Environmental Recovery
    Presented by Dr. Abe Leguyhes
    Lead Anarchivist, International Republic of Scholars and Scientists
    McMurdo City, Antarctica

To say that we once knew more, so much more than we do now, is almost a truism. Still, I speak with confidence when I say that the discovery of Angel-R will stand as one of the most important finds of the past 50 years. Not since we first located the island of Silica Vali and deciphered its California Data Cloud have we been able to reconstruct such an accurate picture of life prior to the Second Dark Age. And what makes the discovery of Angel-R such a triumph is that this

Angel was extremely well-preserved and in near-working condition, as if she had been maintained by someone for quite some time. Just who such a person could have been is unknown, but it could very well have been Clayton or even Beagel himself, and if any other anarchivist here wants to earn the gratitude of everyone present by choosing to follow this lead, go forward in full faith, hope, and scholarly confidence.

Still, I digress, and my earlier statement bears repeating. Since we now have a nearly complete Angel in our possession, the knowledge I and my fellow team of anarchivists have uncovered will be invaluable to understanding the Profit Wars and the events immediately preceding the Great Grid Collapse. Angel-R's meticulous logs allow us insight into perhaps the greatest mystery of our generation: why we once lost our language, how it suddenly returned, and how we can one day arrive at Beagel's pure tongue—what history has described as the langaj of language and life itself.

The multimedicines among you, skeptics that you rightfully are, may ask what makes Angel-R so unique. After all, Angel-N was also discovered nearly intact, and he taught us much about the high level of biotechnological advancement achieved during the age of corporatocracy, but it's now clear that while we learned much about Angel physiology when examining Angel-N, in learning it, we likely destroyed him. What we did not then understand was the importance of silk circuitry, and without a Beagel to guide us, we were left with an Angel who could act, but could not think. The damage we did to Angel-N's neural patterns was too great, and our knowledge of Angel repair and wetworks too limited, to fully understand how or why Angels played such an important role in pre-Collapse society.

All to say that Angel-R represents a breakthrough of significant proportions, and yet this particular Angel is not without her problems. We were unable to compensate for the severe corrosion of her visual receptors—perhaps if we again master stem cell technology as a means of bodily repair, we can—so videographic evidence was impossible to recover. Therefore the Angel-R archive is primarily one of sound, speech, and text, as you shall soon see. Regardless, the wetwork processors of Angel-R are in extremely good condition, and now that we have been able to access her distinct neural patterns as well as link her to the California Data Cloud, we've learned a great deal. What we found when studying the Angel-R logs is that for every action or incident she was directly involved in, Angel-R produced a narrative, a counter-narrative, and what we've termed an "alternarrative": an additional log that was confined to her subconscious but could be shared among other Angels through the web. This quickly became known as *Lingua Angelica*: the language of a doubled, double consciousness. The result is that the Angels were capable of examining the world from multiple perspectives, telling a story in multiple ways at once, and in this capacity they surpassed their contemporary human counterparts.

In other words, Angels were often aware of things most humans who lived in the incorporated nation-states were not. Having a neural wetwork meant that Angels had free, unfettered access to information, and given that information was categorized as a commodity during the age of corporatocracy, Angel-R's ability to present us with historical contexts and referents has already changed our understanding of life during the Profit Wars of the incorporated nation-states. The fact that Angel-R's alternarrative acts as a meta-commentary, sometimes contextualizing, sometimes describing, sometimes challenging the supposed reason for events as they happened, as well as simultaneously alluding to other historical documents, has helped us to better understand not only how the normal citizens of the incorporated nation-states spoke, but also how those communications fit into the pattern of intentional semantic change that began well before the worldwide socio-economic transition to the incorporated nation-state itself, a drift that perhaps started, by my own estimate, as early as the late twentieth century.

Yet I get ahead of myself. I sometimes do that, too. By cross-referencing Angel-R's logs with earlier records recovered from the California Data Cloud, we found that Angel-R's alternarrative contains numerous quotes and passages, some only slightly altered, from the following sources and individuals: Kathy Acker, Samuel Beckett, Madison Smartt Bell, the King James Bible, David Bowie, James Brown, Italo

Calvino, Albert Camus, George Clinton, De La
Soul, Ralph Ellison, Percival Everett, Jean-
Claude Forest, E. M. Forster, Gustave Flaubert,
Flavor Flav, William Gaddis, William Gass,
Anna Graham, Vera Henross, Hilda Hilst,
Johnny Horton, Gregory Jacobs (aka Edward
Ellington Humphrey III), William James, Prince
Jazzbo (aka Linval Roy Carter), Linton Kwesi
Johnson, Jamaica Kincaid, David Lawrence, Jo
Li, Liberace, David Markson, Bob Marley, Talat
Mehmood, Wolfgang Amadeus Mozart, John
Dos Passos, Lee "Scratch" Perry, Marcel Proust,
Thomas Pynchon, Bertrand Russell, Mike Skin-
ner, Stendahl, Gerald Stern, Lynne Tillman,
Tom Tom Club, Walt Whitman, Ludwig
Wittgenstein, Karen Tei Yamashita, Thomas
Yorke, and perhaps several others whom we've
yet to identify.

Such a list is so long and varied that I'll leave
it to those present who specialize in pre-Grego-
rian Calendar Gap research, contentious schol-
ars-in-arms though you be, to conduct your
inquiries into both their individual and collective
significance. But for those among us who strive
to resurrect Beagel's living langaj, what is
perhaps most important about this list of names
is that it provides us with clues, insight into why
the forebears of the corporatocracy found it
necessary to mandate semantic change, as much
as it gives us a means of understanding how the
language of one age gave rise to a complete
semantic shift and the economic attempt to
control language in the next. And thus, while our
knowledge of the age of corporatocracy and the

incorporated nation-states is by no means complete, we can now start to establish a cultural-linguistic timeline of the world prior to the Great Grid Collapse and the Second Dark Age.

Furthermore, we now have a greater breadth and depth of detail, a way of reconstructing the world's timeline throughout the Profit Wars era, when the incorporated nation-states abandoned the Gregorian calendar in favor of recording history according to swings in the major world markets: what is colloquially referred to as the Dow cycles. During those years, or potentially decades, there were few verdant places left, and previous videographic and oral evidence confirms that the incorporated nation-states were highly-congested, heavily-industrialized environments. Most food and goods were artificially manufactured, since artificial materials were considered "civilized"—a catch-all word used to indicate the ideological correctness of the corporatocracy. We can now definitively prove that the Earth of the Profit Wars was one where any sort of uninhabited green space was seen as underutilized land that needed to be managed and exploited for its economic potential, with its citizens viewed as backwards, lazy primitives, guilty of sloth, and thus the few territories around the world that still possessed open fields and farms, mineral-rich or arable land of any sort, were often the targets of the various incorporated nation-states' troops. It has been proven before, notably in the works of my predecessor, the great anarchivist Dr. G. Baylee Shue, but vegetation, especially vegetation that grew unregulated and was not somehow sold for profit, was anathema. For more than this singular reason, we strive to contact Beagel and learn his langaj and we gather as much evidence as we can, for only then can we ever complete our work of bettering the world by reminding ourselves of the mistakes of our past, so as not to repeat them. Angel-R is but one small step in the right direction.

Equally as important, Angel-R has given us unequivocal evidence that silverfish were not the mythical beasts we once believed them to be. Such a thing bears repeating: Silverfish were real. Perhaps they were one of the many species lost to the Profit Wars' extinction-level calamities, but at the very least, the detailed logs of Angel-R give us insight into basic silverfish physical appearance and diet. They appear to have been technovores, wetworked creatures that consumed electric energy, and therefore likely died out after the Great Grid Collapse. In addition, we now know that the legendary Dr. Beagel, whose figure still looms as large as it does enigmatic, wielded considerable influence over silverfish, although it is unclear whether or not his influence waxed and waned over time, and exactly how his influence came to be. Surely we can all lament the fact that not much evidence regarding Dr. Beagel survived the Second Dark Age, for the Angel-R record indicates that he played no small part in the creation of both the Angels and silverfish, and set about to encounter his creations on more than one occasion. Nonetheless, while we are still examining his encounter with Angel-R for more clues, our preliminary findings have been quite hopeful, in that they give us hints as to his location. Still, Beagel is legendary for being a trickster and, as it's often said, he may one day find us, should we ever stop looking. Alas, our investigations must remain incomplete until we are provided with further definitive evidence.

Yet I am a man of faith, and I am confident that Beagel is still out there, somehow orchestrating our discoveries and actions with most of us none the wiser. A minority opinion, granted, so let us agree to disagree on the matter while we nonetheless have much work left to do. Regardless of whether or not Beagel returns, or when he returns, or if we one day find him, our work to rebuild remains, because it's by our ability to reconstruct and understand the events of the past that we can perhaps revise our future, especially given that despite our scholastic and semantic differences, we're now all in agreement that, this time, instead of reshaping the planet, we will restore it. Therefore, on behalf of my entire team, I dither no longer and instead present the Angel-R archive in its entirety. Thank you...

Well, perhaps I spoke too soon. If you all would, please, just be so kind as to give me a moment while I inquire of my assistant. Are we ready? Is it on...?

Dédicaces

Since there are so many people who played a hand in the development of both me and this book, I must give credit where credit is due. First and foremost, the biggest thanks of all to goes to my mom, Camille Shavers. Not only did she raise me, but she also had to put up with so much of my self-serving and self-absorbed bull-shit throughout the years that she deserves every superlative and accolade. I love you, mom. And for my dad, Ronald Shavers, because you're my best friend. I love you, too. And to my brothers, thanks for always having my back: Anthony Robinson, Mario Eberle, and my brother from another mother, Jeffery N. Black.

To my teachers, professors, and unofficial mentors. Big props to you all, because your insights continue to influence me, even when what I learned sometimes comes out sideways: Ms. Paris, Dr. Thurn, Mrs. Miller, Phoebe Chao, John Smyth, Maura Spiegel, Philip Lopate,

Gladden Schrock, Geoffrey O'Brien, Sharon Holland, Nick Brown, Madhu Dubey, Walter Benn Michaels, and Joe Tabbi. Special thanks to Jeffery Renard Allen, for changing the trajectory of my life, and to Cris Mazza, for repeatedly emphasizing that all my dime store philosophy would go down better if I only just added something as stupid as a few knock-knock jokes. Thanks to every single one of you.

To my creative friends-in-arms, who totally know what it's like to make a "beautiful mess." Thanks to Rob Arnold, Christina Chiu, Eurie Dahn, David Ebenbach, Matthew Jakubowski, Elizabeth Kelly, Michael Moreci, Daniel Nester, Alan Michael Parker, Susan Steinberg, Lex Williford, and Barbara Ungar. Also, to Jericho Brown, Krista Franklin, Duriel Harris, Davida Ingram, Tyhembia Jess, Doug Kearney, John Keene, Tashi Ko, Toni Asante Lightfoot, and the entire crew of the Second Sun Salon and *Callaloo* Creative Writing Workshops: You folks have served as my inspiration for far too long to note. For the sage advice, motivation, and eleventh-hour saves, special thanks to Sawako Nakayasu, Krista Caballero, and Corinna Cape. And of course, thanks to Kenyatta JP Garcia for being the one to set everything in motion. Here's looking to when it comes back again.

This book was made wholly possible by the generous gifts of uninterrupted time and space in which to work, revise, and relax in aesthetically and intellectually stimulating locales. Thank you, Lesley Williamson and staff of the Constance Saltonstall Foundation for the Arts in

Ithaca, New York; and thank you, Sheila Pleasants and the entire staff at the Virginia Center for the Creative Arts in Amherst, Virginia. The fruits of my labor are a direct result of your labor. Thank you so very much.

And finally, if there is anyone I've missed or neglected to mention in my spastic shout-out, well then, please forgive me. Sometimes I get ahead of myself. Naturally, it's just an error of omission that we'll rectify come second iteration.

Photo credit Rob O'Neil

Rone Shavers is a writer who publishes in multiple genres. His fiction has appeared in various journals, including *Another Chicago Magazine*, *Big Other*, *Identity Theory*, *PANK*, and *The Operating System*. Shavers' non-fiction essays and essay-length reviews have appeared in such diverse publications as *American Book Review*, *BOMB*, *Electronic Book Review*, *Fiction Writers Review*, and *The Quarterly Conversation*.

Shavers has been awarded artist-in-residence fellowships to the *Callaloo* Creative Writing Workshops, the MacDowell Colony, the Ragdale Arts Foundation, the Constance Saltonstall Foundation for the Arts, the Virginia Center for the Creative Arts, and Vermont Studio Center. He teaches courses in fiction and contemporary literature at The College of Saint Rose in Albany, New York. *Silverfish* is his first novel.

ALSO BY CLASH BOOKS

GIRL LIKE A BOMB

Autumn Christian

CENOTE CITY

Monique Quintana

THIS BOOK IS BROUGHT TO YOU BY MY STUDENT LOANS

Megan J. Kaleita

ARSENAL/SIN DOCUMENTOS

Francesco Levato

TRY NOT TO THINK BAD THOUGHTS

Art by Matthew Revert

JAH HILLS

Unathi Slasha

NEW VERONIA

M.S. Coe

COMAVILLE

Kevin Bigley

DARK MOONS RISING IN A STARLESS NIGHT

Mame Bougouma Diene

WE PUT THE LIT IN LITERARY

CL◀SH

CLASHBOOKS.COM

FOLLOW US ON TWITTER, IG & FB

@clashbooks

EMAIL

clashmediabooks@gmail.com

Printed in the USA
CPSIA information can be obtained
at www.ICGtesting.com
JSHW012056140824
68134JS00035B/3466

9 781944 866747